This book was inspired by our dog Rescue, who lived the first 10 months of her life in a shelter waiting for a family of her own.

Thank you to all the men, women and organizations that work around the clock to rescue animals in need.

There are many great local groups within the area I live. I was introduced to Canon's Cause through the vet clinic my husband and I use in the town of Caledonia where we live. They rescue, heal, foster and find forever homes for dogs and sometimes cats. We were lucky to adopt one of our cats from them. They provided the medical and surgical care she needed, cleaned her, cared for her and gave her a safe place to heal. We saw her on their Facebook page when she was ready to be adopted and knew she belonged in our family.

Please think of your local organizations if you are ever looking to adopt a new fur baby. If you are unable to adopt, please consider fostering, sponsoring, donating or educating others.

ISBN: 978-1-989506-21-9

The Publisher, associates, authors, illustrators, design team, distributors, and partners, will not be responsible or liable for any allergic reactions, adverse effects, including death, from the recipe included therein. Please note that Xylitol is fatal for animals and should NOT be used in the recipe, as indicated on the page containing the ingredients.

Published in Canada by Pandamonium Publishing House™.
www.pandamoniumpublishing.com
pandapublishing8@gmail.com

Design: Emily James
Cover Design: Emily James
emilyjamesillustration.com

This book is dedicated to:

My parents Ray and Gayle, who always encouraged reading, creativity and a belief that anything is possible if you try. My love of storytelling comes from growing up listening to my dad make up tales and poems. One day I may even be able to use one of his opening line suggestions.

My son Brandon and daughter Cari, who welcomed me into their lives, made me a mom, and filled our home with love and laughter.
I am so proud of you both.

My husband Stacey: the man who laughs when he is crowded by our two cats and two dogs, and who always supports every new idea and hobby I have, even with my closet full of forgotten ones. Thank you for believing in me and my dream to be an author.
You are my rock, my heart, my love.

TWELVE DAYS OF RESCUE

written by
Tonya Cartmell

illustrated by
Emily James

Sitting all alone in a cold, dark cage at the very back of the animal shelter, was a small, sad dog.

She had long floppy ears that looked too large for her head and big golden-brown eyes. Her fur was mostly black with a white diamond on her chest. She had light brown fur on her lower legs and paws that made it look like she was wearing socks. The staff at the shelter named her Socks because her legs looked so cute.

Socks was almost one year old and had lived in the shelter since she was born. The staff tried hard to make her smile. They were all very nice to Socks, and even gave her extra treats. But nothing they did could make Socks smile.

Every night Socks dreamed of having a family of her own. Her paws moved in her sleep as she chased the balls they threw, and her quiet dream barks of excitement could be heard by the other animals.

When families came into the shelter to adopt a dog, Socks didn't jump and bark like the other dogs when people walked by her cage. She just sat quietly, wishing someone would notice her and take her home. She kept hoping the family in her dreams would come.

One day, her wish came true when a family stopped at her cage and called her name. Socks wagged her tail, wiggled her whole body and gave them a big doggy smile because she knew she finally had a family of her own. Socks was so excited to be going home with her family.

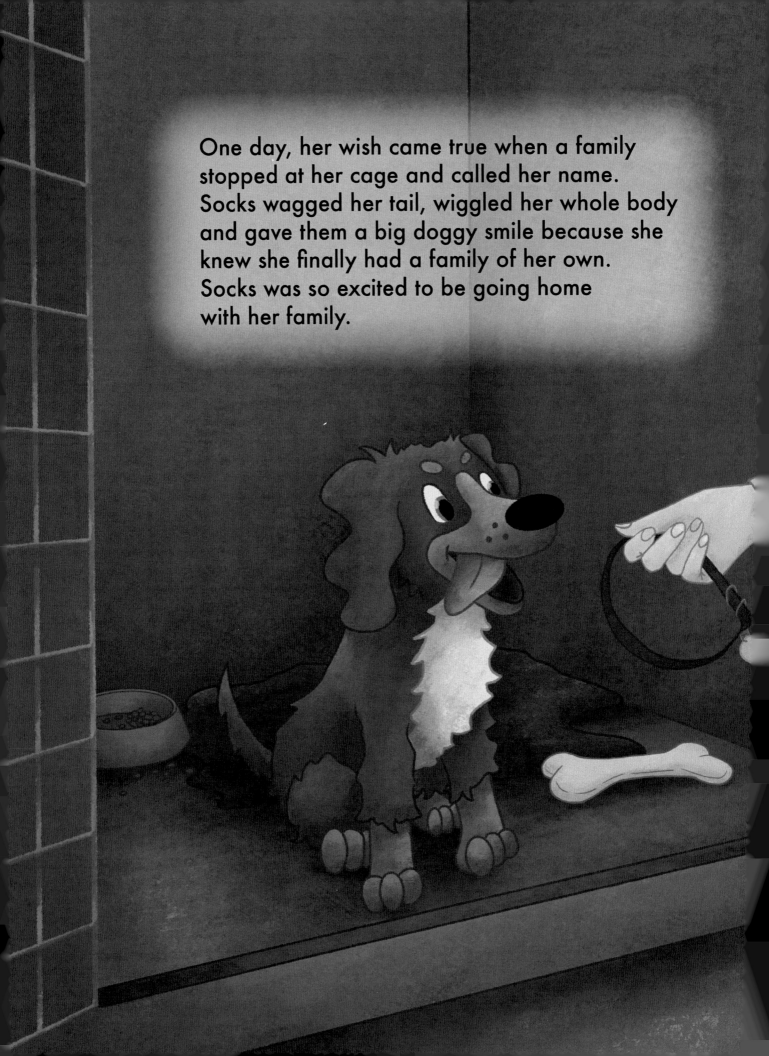

Over the first twelve days in her new home, Socks kept track of all the wonderful things that came from being in a family.

She called it
"The Twelve Days of Rescue"
and it went like this.

On the first day of rescue,
my family gave to me;
a home filled with
lots of love.

On the second day of rescue,
my family gave to me;
2 shiny bowls,
and a home filled with
lots of love.

On the third day of rescue,
my family gave to me;
3 soft beds,
2 shiny bowls,
and a home filled with
lots of love.

On the fourth day of rescue,
my family gave to me;
4 walks a day,
3 soft beds,
2 shiny bowls,
and a home filled with
lots of love.

On the fifth day of rescue,
my family gave to me;
5 water swims,
4 walks a day,
3 soft beds,
2 shiny bowls,
and a home filled with
lots of love.

On the sixth day of rescue, my family gave to me;
6 fancy collars,
5 water swims,
4 walks a day,
3 soft beds,
2 shiny bowls,
and a home filled with lots of love.

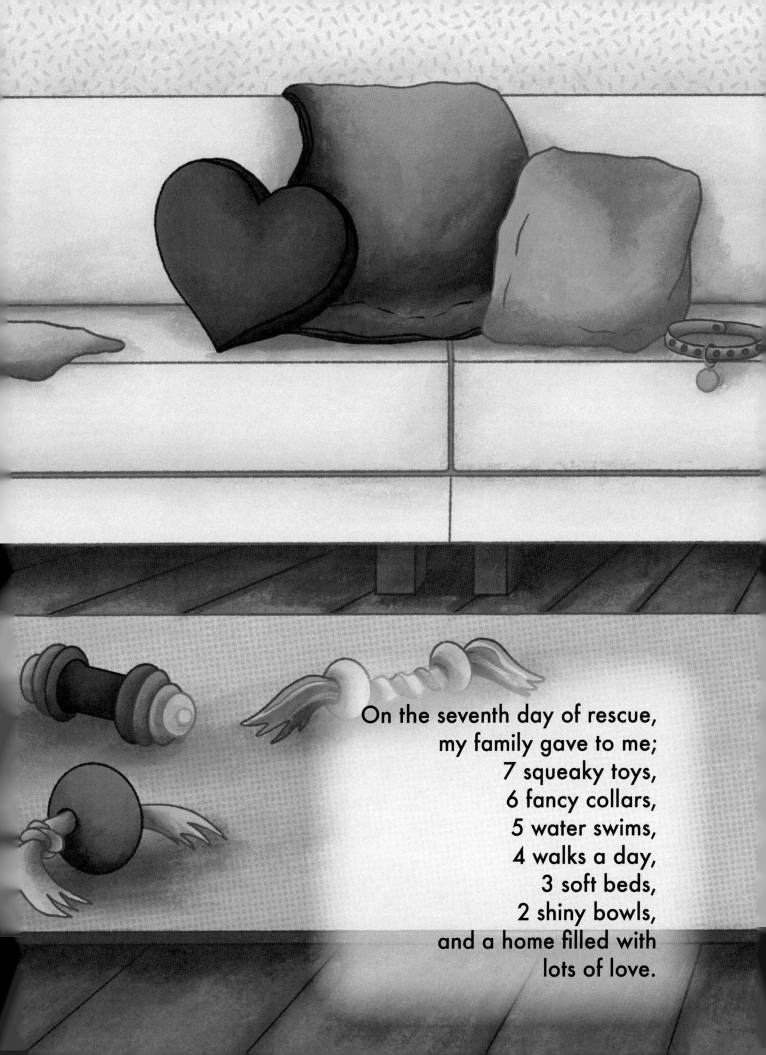

On the seventh day of rescue,
my family gave to me;
7 squeaky toys,
6 fancy collars,
5 water swims,
4 walks a day,
3 soft beds,
2 shiny bowls,
and a home filled with
lots of love.

On the eighth day of rescue,
my family gave to me;
8 hugs and kisses,
7 squeaky toys,
6 fancy collars,
5 water swims,
4 walks a day,
3 soft beds,
2 shiny bowls,
and a home filled with
lots of love.

On the ninth day of rescue,
my family gave to me;
9 crunchy cookies,
8 hugs and kisses,
7 squeaky toys,
6 fancy collars,
5 water swims,
4 walks a day,
3 soft beds,
2 shiny bowls,
and a home filled with
lots of love.

On the tenth day of rescue,
my family gave to me;
10 belly scratches,
9 crunchy cookies,
8 hugs and kisses,
7 squeaky toys,
6 fancy collars,
5 water swims,
4 walks a day,
3 soft beds,
2 shiny bowls,
and a home filled
with lots of love.

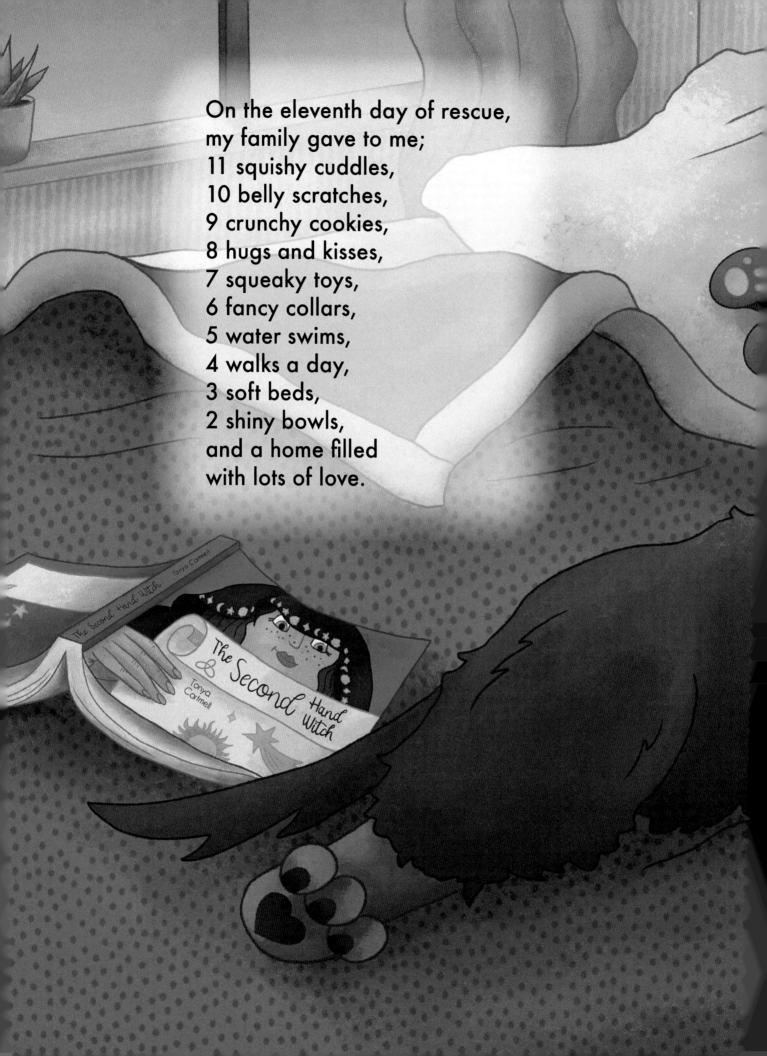

On the eleventh day of rescue,
my family gave to me;
11 squishy cuddles,
10 belly scratches,
9 crunchy cookies,
8 hugs and kisses,
7 squeaky toys,
6 fancy collars,
5 water swims,
4 walks a day,
3 soft beds,
2 shiny bowls,
and a home filled
with lots of love.

On the twelfth day of rescue,
my family gave to me;
12 bouncy balls
11 squishy cuddles,
10 belly scratches,
9 crunchy cookies,
8 hugs and kisses,
7 squeaky toys,
6 fancy collars,
5 water swims,
4 walks a day,
3 soft beds,
2 shiny bowls,
and a home filled
with lots of love.

Socks was so happy that she finally had a family of her own; she smiled, always wagged her tail, and gave them lots of doggy kisses.

When she laid down to sleep on one of her soft beds each night, Socks wished that all the other shelter animals would get to have their own Twelve Days of Rescue too.

Rescue's Recipe for Tasty Treats

Ingredients

- 2 cups flour (can substitute rolled oats/gluten free rolled oats)
- 1 cup canned pumpkin
- 1/2 cup peanut butter (natural is best, do NOT use peanut butter that contains xylitol, as this ingredient can be fatal to dogs)

Directions

1. Preheat oven to 375 F.
2. Mix the pumpkin & peanut butter together in a large bowl.
3. Stir in the flour/oats and combine the mixture until dough forms.
4. Roll out the dough onto a lightly floured surface (use more oats if your pup is gluten free).
5. Cut into shapes with a cookie cutter or a knife.
6. Place treats onto an ungreased baking sheet (allow half inch pace for expansion while baking).
7. Bake for 12 minutes.
9. Allow to cool.
10. Let your dog enjoy!

This recipe makes approximately 60 treats using a small sized cookie cutter. We keep 20 treats in a jar at a time (1 week long shelf life) and freeze the rest!

Emily James is a Canadian illustrator and designer from the small town of Newcastle, Ontario. She loves creating playful visuals both digitally and traditionally while incorporating a variety of colours and textures.

She is currently working to obtain her Honours Bachelor of Illustration at Sheridan College. When she is not drawing, you can probably spot Emily playing with her dog Bailey, reading a good book or spending time with her friends and family.

www.emilyjamesillustration.com
@ej_illustrations